The Day Miss Spicey Waggled Her Tail Off

JAMES W. HOLMES

DEDICATION

This book is dedicated to the memory of
our original "Three Bears":
Papa Sugar Bear Holmes ("Shug"),
Mama Spice Bear Holmes ("Miss Spicey") and
Baby Pepper Bear Holmes ("Peppy Sue").
They have all three left us, but will live in
our hearts forever.

ACKNOWLEDGMENTS

Special thanks to Michael A. Stell, Illustrator,
and to Dr. Pat Mims, Veterinarian,
who took care of all of our Three Bears for
their whole lives.

Grandpa Jim had said it at least a thousand times. Everybody had heard it: "Miss Spicey, one of these days, you're gonna waggle that tail completely off!" Then he'd let out a big "grandpa" laugh and scratch Miss Spicey's ears affectionately.

But nobody really worried about it happening, of course — nobody, that is, except Little Ben. And he didn't tell anybody he worried about it.

You see, Miss Spicey, the family's female Shih Tzu puppy, was always so happy to see Little Ben that she wagged her tail furiously every time he came around.

And Little Ben had not yet learned that Grandpa Jim, on occasion, at least, tended to exaggerate things.

So he worried about it — a lot!

But still, he didn't tell anybody.

The day it "really" happened, Little Ben and Miss Spicey had played together for hours in the yard outside and on the rug inside, and both were tired out and ready for naptime. So Little Ben went into his bedroom, while Miss Spicey headed for her bed in Grandpa Jim's room.

It was a cool, quiet day, and the entire family was napping.

Then Little Ben felt a scratching at the side of his bed and looked over to see Miss Spicey there, her tail waggling more furiously than ever. She wanted to play some more.

"Miss Spicey," said Little Ben, "you know what Grandpa Jim said — if you keep waggling your tail so hard and fast, one of these days, you're gonna waggle it completely off. Stop waggling so hard!"

WHUMP!

But when she heard Little Ben's voice and saw him looking at her, Miss Spicey just turned up the speed on her waggling tail, and, all of a sudden, Little Ben saw it fly completely off and hit the bedroom wall with a "WHUMP!" Little Ben looked in horror at poor Miss Spicey's tail lying on the carpet near the wall. Miss Spicey was still jumping up and down, wanting to play, not even aware that she had finally waggled her tail off.

Little Ben quickly jumped out of bed, ran over and picked up Miss Spicey's waggled-off tail, then stood there, looking at it, while tears welled up in his eyes. Then he looked down at Miss Spicey and exclaimed: "Now you've done it, Miss Spicey! You did just what Grandpa Jim said you were going to do! How will I ever get your tail back on? You can't go around without your tail!"

Then Little Ben remembered the Scotch tape. Only the day before, he'd watched Grandpa Jim use it to repair a broken crayon. "The Scotch tape!" he said to himself and to Miss Spicey. So he hurried to the kitchen drawer where the Scotch tape was stored, then slipped quietly back into his bedroom with the now-tailless Miss Spicey right behind him.

Working frantically, he positioned Miss Spicey's tail as well as he could and wrapped Scotch tape around it to secure it to her body. It drooped a little, but at least it stayed in place.

But it just hung there. There was no longer any waggle in it at all!

Little Ben started to cry.

Suddenly, he heard his mother's voice: "Benji," she said, "time to get up! You shouldn't nap all day, or you won't be able to sleep tonight."

When he came into the kitchen rubbing his eyes and crying, his mother was alarmed.

Miss Spicey was gone, and Little Ben didn't know where she was.

"What's wrong, Benji?" she asked. "Why are you crying?"

So Little Ben told his mother the whole, sad story. He was especially sad that Miss Spicey's tail would no longer waggle, he said. That was the cutest part about her, and now he would never see it again.

Taking Little Ben in her arms, his mother drew him to her and smilingly tried to explain that he had only dreamed the whole thing while he was taking his nap, that it wasn't even possible for Miss Spicey to completely waggle her tail off, and that Grandpa Jim was always exaggerating things just for the fun of it.

She had just about convinced him that the whole thing was a bad dream when Miss Spicey came mini-galloping into the kitchen, jumping up and down at the sight of Little Ben, her tail waggling at near-supersonic speed.

"See, Benji!" said his mother, as Little Ben quickly got down to greet Miss Spicey. "I told you the whole thing was a bad dream. Miss Spicey's just fine!"

Then they both noticed the Scotch tape around Miss Spicey's tail.

His mother was surprised and mystified, but Little Ben exclaimed: "Mom, it worked after all! It just took a little while!"

About that time, Grandpa Jim, up from his nap, came into the kitchen. He asked what was going on, and Little Ben told the story again, as Miss Spicey jumped and waggled her tail.

When he'd heard everything, Grandpa Jim laughed heartily, rubbed both Little Ben and Miss Spicey on the head, and sent an amused glance in the direction of Little Ben's mother, who was still sitting in her chair with a strange look on her face.

Then he walked over and put something in the kitchen drawer while nobody was looking his way, all the while chuckling to himself that he'd now heard the whole story twice.

So it's still a mystery how Miss Spicey's tail got waggled off and then Scotch-taped back on that day.

Only one person knows the full story — and, as he says, with his big laugh,

"I'm not telling!"